2:

Friends
Are
Forever

Let's
PlayHouse

Written by Emma Quay

Illustrated by Anna Walker

SCHOLASTIC

For Gabrielle ~ EQ
For Bonnie and Scarlett ~ AW

First published in 2009 by Scholastic Australia

This edition first published in 2010 by Scholastic Children's Books

Euston House, 24 Eversholt Street

London NW1 1DB

a division of Scholastic Ltd

www.scholastic.co.uk

London ~ New York ~ Toronto ~ Sydney ~ Auckland

Mexico City ~ New Delhi ~ Hong Kong

www.emmaquay.com

www.annawalker.com.au

ISBN 978 1407 12077 5

Hello, Panda.

Hello, Sheep.

Hello, Owl.

All together . . . friends are forever.

"Let's play house,"
says Owl.

"Put that chair over there,"
says Panda.

"Catch the other end of the blanket," says Sheep.

"Knock, knock.
Can I come in?"
says Owl.

"It's too squashy,"
says Sheep.

"You're sitting on my tail," says Owl.

"I'm getting out,"
says Panda.

"Oh, Panda!" say Sheep and Owl.
"You've taken the roof!"

"I'm not Panda," says Panda.
"I'm a jellyfish."

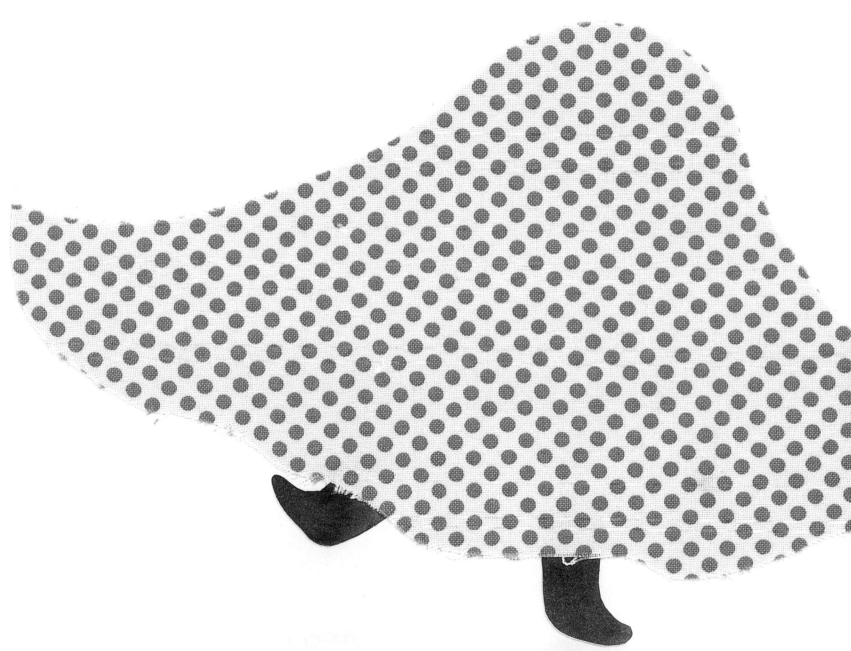

"I'm a jellyfish too,"
says Sheep.

"So am I,"
says Owl.

"Blob,   blob!"

blob,

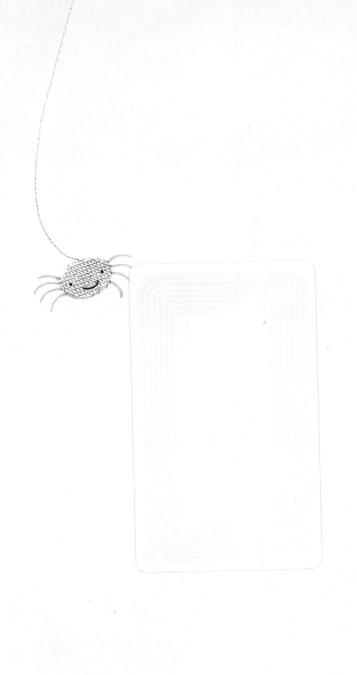